MR. MEN
ADVENTURE ON
WHEELS

Original concept by
Roger Hargreaves

Written and illustrated by
Adam Hargreaves

It was a remarkably odd day for Mr Busy.

He had got up early, as usual, got washed, brushed his teeth, eaten his breakfast and cleaned the house from top to bottom, as usual, then discovered that he had nothing to do.

Everything on his 'to do' list had been crossed off.

Mr Busy sat at his kitchen table and looked at the clock.

What was he going to do for a whole day?

And then it occurred to him.

He would do nothing.

He would have a day doing nothing at the beach.

As the sun rose, Mr Busy set off in his car. He soon reached a building site.

Mr Uppity was building a new house for himself.

Mr Uppity already had a house. A huge house.

But he wanted an even bigger house.

The building site was in chaos.

Mr Wrong had dug a hole with his digger. But he had dug it in the wrong place.

Mr Uppity was furious.

Mr Forgetful had forgotten to turn off his cement mixer.
And Mr Uppity was even more furious about that!

Mr Busy looked at the chaos. He thought about his plan to
do nothing for the day. But he just could not help himself.

He had to get involved.

He had to get busy!

So he got busy sorting everything out with a bulldozer.

And being the busy fellow he is, he soon had everything finished.

Mr Busy waved goodbye and continued on his way to the beach.

Outside the fire station, the fire crew were all standing on the pavement looking very worried.

Little Miss Quick, who drove the fire engine, had been in such a hurry to leave when the alarm had rung that she had driven off before the fire crew could get on board.

Mr Busy gave the fire crew a lift to the fire. The beach could wait. There was plenty of the day left to do nothing.

As he watched the fire crew putting out the fire, he heard a sudden cry of pain.

"OW! I've burnt my ..." began Mr Bump.

"Don't worry!" cried Mr Busy.

And without letting Mr Bump finish his sentence, Mr Busy bundled him into the back of an ambulance and drove him to the hospital with the siren ringing.

However, on the way they got stuck behind Mr Slow and his steamroller so Mr Busy took a shortcut ...

... across the fields!

It was a very bumped about Mr Bump who arrived at the hospital.

And it turned out, after all, that Mr Bump had only burnt his tongue on a cup of hot tea.

After leaving the hospital, Mr Busy set off for the beach.

Again.

But along the way, he spotted a very puzzled Mr Funny next to a pile of red noses outside his red nose factory.

Mr Funny's worker, Little Miss Late, was late for work.

Mr Busy quickly got to work packing the red noses in boxes.

Then he loaded the boxes into Mr Funny's delivery lorry using a forklift truck.

Mr. Funny's World of Red Noses

Then Mr Busy drove Mr Funny's delivery lorry to the shop.

Just look at Mr Funny's car!

Mr Funny thanked him for all his help and with a big smile on his face, Mr Busy continued his journey to the beach.

Over a hedge he saw Farmer Field's farm.

It was the busiest time of the year on the farm and Farmer Field needed all the help he could get.

However, the help that he had got was no help at all.

Mr Muddle had tipped the grain into the pigsty.

And Little Miss Scatterbrain was trying to plough the pond!

Mr Busy knew just what was needed.

A tow truck.

In no time at all, Mr Busy had sorted out the mess.

He decided he even had time to harvest the field of barley before he went to the beach!

Mr Busy was about to reach the beach, he could even see it.

But it was on the other side of a racetrack.

A racetrack where Mr Rush was looking for someone to race with.

And busy old Mr Busy just could not resist the challenge.

Mr Rush climbed onto his motorbike and Mr Busy got into a racing car.

On the count of three, they were off.

Mr Rush was the fastest thing on two legs and he thought he was also the fastest thing on two wheels.

But Mr Busy was even faster on four wheels.

He sped past Mr Rush and over the finish line first.

But he didn't stop there, he raced on out of the racetrack to the beach.

Mr Busy had finally arrived.

But the sun was setting and it was time to go home.

So much for Mr Busy's day of doing absolutely nothing!